3 4028 07959 4488
HARRIS COUNTY PUBLIC LIBRARY

JPIC Steink
Steinkellner, Elisabeth
My new granny
$16.95
ocn783160131
11/20/2012

D1413591

Copyright © 2012 by Elisabeth Steinkellner and Michael Roher
Originally published in Austria as *Die neue Omi* copyright © 2011 by Verlag Jungbrunnen Wien

All Rights Reserved. No part of this book may be reproduced in any manner without the express written consent of the publisher, except in the case of brief excerpts in critical reviews or articles. All inquiries should be addressed to Sky Pony Press, 307 West 36th Street, 11th Floor, New York, NY 10018.

Sky Pony Press books may be purchased in bulk at special discounts for sales promotion, corporate gifts, fund-raising, or educational purposes. Special editions can also be created to specifications. For details, contact the Special Sales Department, Sky Pony Press, 307 West 36th Street, 11th Floor, New York, NY 10018 or info@skyhorsepublishing.com.

Sky Pony® is a registered trademark of Skyhorse Publishing, Inc.®, a Delaware corporation.

Visit our website at www.skyponypress.com.

10 9 8 7 6 5 4 3 2 1

Manufactured in China, May 2012
This product conforms to CPSIA 2008

Library of Congress Cataloging-in-Publication Data

Steinkellner, Elisabeth.
[Die neue Omi. English]
My new granny / Elisabeth Steinkellner ; illustrated by Michael Roher.
p. cm.
Summary: Fini's grandmother used to travel, cook, and fuss over Fini's hair but since she came home from the hospital Granny is like a different person, and Fini must learn how to love her just the same.
ISBN 978-1-62087-223-9 (hardcover : alk. paper)
[1. Grandmothers--Fiction. 2. Old age--Fiction. 3. Alzheimer's disease--Fiction. 4. Family life--Fiction.] I. Roher, Michael, ill. II. Title.
PZ7.S82643My 2012
[E]--dc23
2012010540

Written by Elisabeth Steinkellner
Illustrated by Michael Roher
Translated by Connie Stradling Morby

My New Granny

Sky Pony Press
New York

My old Granny always made a fuss about my hairdo.

"Fini, what have you done to your beautiful hair again?" she sighed and shook her head, not understanding.

Then she covered my head with a hat and went to the park with me. We fed the ducks and dreamed about faraway places. My old Granny took a lot of trips and sent me postcards from all over. And when she was back home again, she always cooked very exotic dishes.

My old Granny was, of course, a really good cook. After a meal at Granny's, Mom and Dad were always in a good mood for the rest of the day.

But then Granny had to go to the hospital and came back as a new Granny.

My new Granny is different.

My new Granny adores my hairdo.

"How pretty you look, Fini!" she says and strokes my hair. My new Granny would rather eat the hard bread crumbs herself instead of feeding them to the ducks.

And taking trips is also something my new Granny can't do anymore. A few weeks ago she packed her suitcases for the last time to move from her apartment to live with Mom, Dad, and me. Now what she likes best is sitting in the armchair in her room and telling me stories about her childhood, smiling and looking out the window with a strange expression.

A few days ago, my new Granny turned on all the burners on the stove, not to cook, but to warm her hands. Since then, there's been a big sign stuck up in the kitchen: "Granny, please don't turn the stove on!" And Mom makes an anxious face and keeps saying, "We all have to keep an eye on Granny, Fini."

Today it's my turn to keep an eye on Granny while Mom is at our neighbor's house. We drink cocoa together, and then I read Granny stories about witches. Granny laughs gleefully, but eventually she closes her eyes and begins to snore. So, I go into my room and organize my crayons.

"Fini!" I suddenly hear Mom call. "Fini, where are you?"

As I come into the kitchen, Granny is lying under the table with her legs spread apart and snoring.

"I was only in my room for a little while," I tell her.

But Mom is angry. "I thought I could trust you, Fini! We agreed that we would all help out."

Granny pops her eyes open and giggles.

"What's so funny about that?" I shout at her. And then I yell at Mom, "Why do I have to take care of Granny? She should take care of herself!"

Mom just flashes me an angry look.

As punishment, tonight I won't be telling Granny a bedtime story.

The next morning, Mom is standing in the living room with a strange woman.

"This is Agatha," Mom explains. "From now on she'll look after Granny for a few hours every day."

I follow Agatha into Granny's room and watch how
she helps her get dressed.

"Hey Agatha," I say, "the doctor at the hospital
said Granny is very lucky that she is even here. It's a
miracle that she woke up again and can stay at home
with us." Agatha smiles and nods.

"You're very lucky," I declare to Granny, and she
laughs and strokes my head.

When Granny is all dressed, I go into the kitchen with her. She sits down and begins to eat her porridge, but the spoon doesn't want to go into her mouth. I watch her for a while, and finally I sit down next to her and we try it together.

Agatha comes and waves a comb. "Time to do your hair!"

"That can be my job," I call out, and Granny nods in agreement.

I love Granny. My new Granny as much as the old one. Now every Sunday morning I'm allowed to do Granny's hair. And then together we admire ourselves in the mirror.

Harris County Public Library
Houston, Texas